THE QUESTION SONG

Kaethe Zemach

Megan Tingley Books

LITTLE, BROWN AND COMPANY

New York · An AOL Time Warner Company

To Heidi, Rachel, and Rebecca, with love.

Thanks to Pat Enslin for inspiration.

First Edition

Library of Congress Cataloging-in-Publication Data

Zemach-Bersin, Kaethe.
    The question song / by Kaethe Zemach.
        p. cm.
    ISBN 0-316-66601-7
    1. Conduct of life – Juvenile literature. [1. Behavior. 2. Conduct of life.] I. Title.

BJ1631 .Z45 2002
398.8 – dc21

2001029351

10 9 8 7 6 5 4 3 2 1

TWP

Printed in Singapore

The illustrations for this book were made with oil paint, hand-cut stencils, and 100% cotton velveteen, in the style of theorem painting, a popular 19th-century decorative art form.
The text was set in Garamond BE, and the display type is hand-lettered by the author.

Most of the day, everything's fine.
We play together and have a nice time.
But once in a while, something goes wrong,
and then we sing The Question Song!

My train is broken! What are we going to do?

My train is broken! What are we going to do?

We'll fix your train
and make it strong.

Then off you go, chugging along!

That's what we will do!

My juice is spilling on the floor! What are we going to do?

My juice is spilling on the floor! What are we going to do?

We'll pick up the cup
and wipe the floor.
Then start again and
pour you some more!

That's what we will do!

I fell down and hurt my knee! What are we going to do?

I fell down and hurt my knee! What are we going to do?

We'll rest until you feel fine.
Then I'll hold your hand,
and you'll hold mine!

That's what we will do!

My shoe came off and fell on the ground! What are we going to do?

My shoe came off and fell on the ground! What are we going to do?

We'll pick up your shoe and
put it on tight.
Then you can swing with all
your might!

That's what we will do!

Look at this, here is another!
One for the sister,
and one for the brother.

That's what we will do!

I can't find my bunny! What are we going to do?

I can't find my bunny! What are we going to do?

We'll look until we find your bunny.

See where she's hiding?
Isn't she funny!

That's what we will do!

My ice cream is melting! What are we going to do?

My ice cream is melting! What are we going to do?

We'll get a cup to catch the drips.
Now gobble it up and lick your lips!

That's what we will do!

It's too high! I can't reach! What are we going to do?

It's too high! I can't reach! What are we going to do?

We'll lift you up. Now you're tall!
Reach your bunny, reach your ball!

That's what we will do!

We'll kiss your toe.
We'll kiss your head.
You have to watch out
if you jump on a bed!

That's what we will do!

Here's an umbrella. Now you're set!
You can play in the rain,
and you won't get wet.

That's what we will do!

We'll take off your coat,
and we'll put on your sweater.
There you go, now you both
feel better!

That's what we will do!

Climb up beside me,
and let's read a book.
What's it about?
Let's take a look.

That's what we will do!

Look at this room! Oh, what a mess! What are we going to do?

We'll pick up the toys and
put them away.
Then we'll have more
room to play.

That's what we will do!

Most of the day, everything's fine.

We play together and have a nice time.

But once in a while,
something goes wrong,
and then we sing
The Question Song!

Oh, that's what we will do!

3-7 feet

6 feet

4 feet

Burrow your heart out!

This can be up to 15 feet of tunneling

GROUNDHOG
SIZE REFERENCE

Approximately 17"

BLUEPRINTS
by
BURR-O-RAMA, INC.
See our ad in the NEW HOG TIMES!

Add some
comfortable
rugs!

5-10 square feet

Don't forget your slippers!

Continue to living section

LIVING QUARTERS